ESCAPE ON YR WYDDFA

Paul Young

Copyright © 2024 Paul Young

All rights reserved

CONTENTS

Title Page	
Copyright	
Chapter One	1
Chapter Two	10
Chapter Three	17
Chapter Four	29
Chapter Five	32
Chapter Six	35
Acknowledgement	45
Praise For Author	47
Books By This Author	49
Seeking Help	51

CHAPTER ONE

Samantha Jones, Sam to everyone but her parents, arrived back at the little cottage at the foot of the mountain.

She had just enough energy left to make herself a hot chocolate before slumping back on the sofa.

She could just see the ridge of the mountain she'd traversed a few hours ago out of the tiny window as she drank.

When she'd finished the enormous mug she placed it on the floor beside the sofa and promptly fell asleep, completely exhausted from a day of climbing Wales' tallest mountain, Yr Wyddfa, or Snowdon as we English like to call it.

The next thing Sam remembered was looking out of the window again to see the cloud previously shrouding just the summit had now descended almost to the valley floor and she could no longer see most of the mountain. The Sun was setting and it was getting dark.

Realising she was still alone in the little cottage, Sam leapt from the sofa, nearly knocking over the empty hot chocolate mug and ran out of the cottage, along the path and through the cleft in the rock that hid the little cottage from the road.

She banged on the door of the neighbouring house.

One of the nice ladies who owned the cottage answered the door.

"Are you OK dear?"

"My husband's not back off the mountain yet. I've been back... well I don't know how long, I fell asleep."

"I'm sure he's fine. Maybe he missed the last bus from Pen-Y-Pass. I'll drive you up there."

"Thank you," said Sam, "I'll get the gate."

The cottage owner drove over the narrow wooden bridge, over the stream below thundering from the previous night's heavy rainfall, and after Sam had closed the wooden gate behind them and got into the passenger seat they turned on to the main road that climbs up through Llanberis pass.

"Shout if you see him dear."

Sam stared out of the window at the passing scenery.

There were just a few other cottages in the first few hundred yards then it was just the mountains on either side dotted with mountain-dwelling sheep with unusually long tails.

There were dry stone walls on both sides of the road which crossed back over the stream and continued uphill. Sam could hear the sound of the engine straining at the seemingly never-ending climb.

Occasionally a lay-by crammed with tourist cars broke up the emptiness of the winding road, some with roof racks laden with camping gear and their boots crammed with luggage. Opposite one lay-by you could see a huge boulder dotted with chalk handprints where earlier in the day Sam had seen people practicing their climbing skills, hanging like monkeys from the underside of the enormous rock.

On the right was the domineering Yr Wyddfa and on the left a huge swathe of giant rocks littered the mountainside, like God had gotten bored of playing with his mountain-scale building blocks and just threw them down the mountainside when his mum told him play time was over.

They all looked completely unstable, like if you moved one they would all come crashing down like the world's biggest game of Jenga.

They soon reached the car park at Pen-Y-Pass, the starting and finishing point of three Snowdon paths, the Pyg track, Miners' track, and the treacherous Crib Goch path.

The car pulled up in the bus turnaround and both women got out. Sam strode off towards the bottom of the Pyg track, a woman on a mission, while the cottage owner headed to the warden post.

There was no sign of her husband, so Sam headed back across the car park.

"I don't see him," Sam called to the cottage owner from a distance as she approached the warden post, slightly out of breath.

"Let's call the mountain rescue then."

It seemed like ages, but within half an hour three distinctive silver Land Rovers of the Llanberis Mountain Rescue Team pulled in to the car park.

"I'm Bryn Davies, Llanberis MRT," announced a six-foot burly Welshman in his high-vis jacket as he jumped out of the first Land Rover, "Who are we missing then?"

"My husband," replied Sam, "Ryan Jones."

"And where did you last see him love?"

"Where the path splits. He wanted to do Crib Goch and I just wanted to come back down Miners so we got separated. He said to come down on my own and he'd meet me back at the cottage."

"Do you know what time that was?"

"I'm not sure, about one maybe."

"Is he an experienced mountaineer your husband?"

"No, we've never climbed before."

"Well Crib Goch is a hard route for anyone. It might just be taking him longer than he thought, but we'll find him. Do you have a photo?"

Crib Goch was indeed a hard route, described as a knife-edged arête, the name means Red Ridge in Welsh, and it is recommended only for experienced mountain walkers. Traversing the route requires an amount of scrambling, using your hands to assist in holds and balance.

"Ryan's got our phone with all our photos on. Sorry, I don't have one, no."

"No problem. Can you describe him for me, and what he's wearing today?"

Sam described her husband Ryan as forty-five, around five foot ten, of medium build, with short dark brown hair and brown eyes. He didn't have any piercings or tattoos. She was sure that he had worn black denim trousers and a polo shirt with black trainers. She couldn't be certain about the colour of his shirt today, but thought it was probably the maroon one. And he had a black and grey backpack with him.

After noting down Sam's description, Bryn walked over to the rest of the team congregated around the Land Rovers and briefed them on the situation.

They all wore high-vis jackets, helmets with head torches, and big backpacks, and two of them carried an orange stretcher between them.

They also had a search and rescue dog, Benji, with them, a black cocker spaniel, trained to find people on the vast expanse of the mountainside, in case Ryan had strayed off the path.

The team of six, plus one dog, headed up the mountain and were soon invisible from the car park due to the now rapidly descending thick cloud.

There were still people coming down off the mountain and the rescue team asked them all if they had seen anyone matching Ryan's description as they passed them.

They called out his name and listened intently for any response, but nothing.

Within an hour the experienced team had reached the start of the razor sharp ridge of Crib Goch.

The official Snowdon paths guide rates Crib Goch 10 out of 10 for both difficulty and fear factor, and recommends it is only used for ascending the mountain as the descent is dangerous.

Normally dogs must be kept on leads on the mountain, so they do not get lost or chase the mountain sheep, but Benji was a trained search and rescue dog. So it was normal for him to be off the lead searching the areas either side of the path.

But for this rescue his trainer, Izzy, was keeping him on the lead and close by as there was dense cloud cover and it was getting darker by the minute. Even though the team were staying fairly close together it was becoming difficult for the person at the back to make out Bryn leading at times.

Just then Benji started barking and the whole group came to an immediate standstill.

Something had caught Benji's attention below them.

Izzy double checked that Benji's reflective collar was secure along with his GPS tracker and LED light around his neck, before unclipping his lead.

Benji took off down the mountainside about forty feet or so away from the path and disappeared behind a large rock jutting out of the ground, before barking again, this time repeatedly.

The mountain rescue team quickly leapt into action, removing their backpacks and pulling out climbing ropes and harnesses.

Bryn Davies and another experienced member of the team put on climbing harnesses, checking each other's harness was secure.

A rope was secured around a suitable rock and Bryn clipped on.

Another of the team reported their status over the radio, "Llanberis MRT, possible sighting of missing hiker, south side of Crib Goch. Bravo Delta is descending now."

Bryn scrambled carefully down the loose rock as the other rescuer in a harness belayed for him.

Once just below the overhanging rock he scrambled across to where Benji was barking from.

Bryn radioed in, "One unconscious male

matching the description, send down the stretcher and call for the helo."

Now that Bryn had located the casualty, Izzy called Benji back up to the path and clipped his lead back on before giving him a huge hug and a treat from the bag around her waist.

"Good boy Benji, well done."

The bright orange stretcher was lowered on a rope next followed by another rescuer to assist Bryn getting the casualty on to the stretcher.

The second rescuer dragged the stretcher under the rock.

"Didn't want to say on the radio," said Bryn quietly to his colleague, "it's not good news."

The two rescuers hauled the lifeless body onto the stretcher and secured him with straps across his chest, waist and legs.

Minutes later the Coastguard search and rescue helicopter could be heard coming up the valley.

Guided by the head torches of the mountain rescue team and using its huge floodlight and infrared cameras the pilot positioned the aircraft directly overhead.

The winch was lowered and Bryn secured it to the stretcher.

"Ready to lift," he called over the radio.

Sam waited patiently at Pen-Y-Pass for news along with a seventh member of the mountain rescue team. They could just about make out the activity on the mountain from the sound of the helicopter and the occasional sweep of its bright light through the clouds.

They had also heard the "Ready to lift" call over the radio.

"Bravo Delta to base," the gruff voice of Bryn Davies came over the radio.

"Go ahead Bryn."

"It's a Delta Charlie, repeat Delta Charlie. Team are returning via Pyg."

Delta Charlie was code for a Deceased Climber. The face of the rescue team member with Sam sank.

"I'm so sorry," she said quietly, "they found a body matching Ryan's description."

Sam fell to her knees, her face in her hands and cried.

CHAPTER TWO

About ten minutes later PC Rebecca Thomas stepped out of her police car, blue lights still flashing after she pulled into the car park at Pen-Y-Pass.

She spoke briefly to the mountain rescue member before approaching Sam, who by now had stopped crying and was leaning against a large concrete block.

"Hello, Mrs. Jones, I'm PC Thomas. I'm very sorry to hear about your husband. The rescuer here needs to wait for the rest of her team to come back down, but I can take you to the hospital where they've taken your husband."

PC Thomas helped Sam into the car, before getting into the driver's seat herself and turning off the blue lights, driving out of the car park and back down the winding Llanberis Pass.

Both women were silent for almost the entire journey to the hospital at Caernarfon, except for one point when the silence was broken by the radio bursting into life.

"Sorry. Let me turn that down," PC Thomas said quietly.

It was completely dark before they reached the hospital and Sam felt bad for the rescuers. She hoped they had all made it down safely from the mountain.

PC Thomas led her inside.

"I think we'd best get you seen first," ushered the PC before explaining the situation to the A&E receptionist.

The waiting room was fairly quiet and the presence of a police officer helped to get Sam seen sooner.

A triage nurse called Sam in to a consulting room while PC Thomas waited outside.

Sam had some scratches on her fingers from the jagged rocks they'd been scaling and blood stains on her hands.

The nurse cleaned them up but there was no need for any dressings.

Noticing a large bruise on Sam's forearm the nurse asked Sam if she wouldn't mind removing her clothes down to her underwear so she could check for further injuries.

There were no more scratches or bleeding, but there were further bruises on Sam's upper arms and a large bruise on her lower back.

"Do you mind if I just take some photos of these bruises?" asked the nurse.

"Er, OK," Sam replied tentatively.

"And then I'd like to get an X-ray taken of this bruised area on your back."

Sam put her trousers and top back on and carried her other clothes.

"Just follow the blue line," instructed the nurse as she handed a green slip of paper to Sam which she had scribbled some indecipherable instructions on for the radiologist.

"Officer," the nurse called after PC Thomas as she got up to follow Sam to the radiology department.

"I've cleaned up the wounds on her fingers, but there's some bruises that don't look consistent with any injury she might have sustained climbing. I'm sending her for an X-ray so the doctor can have a closer look. When her results are back can you come see me again?"

"Sure, OK," replied Rebecca with some intrigue.

The X-ray of Sam's back was quick and painless and she was soon sitting back in the waiting room.

Just ten minutes later the triage nurse called Sam back into the consulting room. Rebecca followed her in this time and there was also a doctor in the room.

"Hi Mrs. Jones, I'm Doctor Suresh, I've been taking a look at your X-rays and I'm pleased to say there's no new damage. However I can see you have had a number of broken ribs in the past, but there's nothing on your NHS record about any previous injuries."

"Oh wow," exclaimed Sam, "that must have been years ago, when I was little. I remember falling down the stairs once but my parents were the type who would just say to dust yourself down and carry on. I'd almost forgotten about it."

"That must be it," replied Doctor Suresh, "you are free to go then. Just take it easy for a few days until those bruises calm down a bit."

He held the consulting room door open for Sam and Rebecca to leave.

In the waiting room, stood just outside the consulting room door waiting for them, was Detective Inspector Peter Constable.

"Mrs. Jones," he introduced himself, "Detective Inspector Peter Constable," emphasising the Inspector.

The irony of his name was not lost on him. He had endured years of torment from his fellow officers during training and probation. It tailed off somewhat once he made Inspector, though he had no doubt that some of the junior officers still made jokes behind his back. He was still a bit nervous when introducing himself so always emphasised Inspector, so as to avoid any confusion.

"Has the doctor given you a clean bill of health?"

"Yes, just a few scrapes and bruises."

"I'm so sorry about your husband but I have to

ask, are you OK to identify the body for us?"

"Yes, yes, of course," replied Sam.

"I'm just going to finish up here with the doctor sir," PC Thomas quickly chipped in.

The DI thought this slightly unusual but carried on anyway escorting Sam to the hospital mortuary.

He rang the bell and waited to be let in.

The mortuary assistant lifted the plain white sheet from the face of the dead body lying on the table in the centre of the room.

"Is this your husband, Mrs. Jones?" asked the DI.

"Yes, that's Ryan."

"Would you like me to leave you for a moment?"

"Yes please."

Sam continued to stare at her husband's lifeless body on the mortuary table.

Peter stepped back out of the mortuary to find PC Thomas waiting for him.

"Rebecca isn't it?"

"Yes sir," confirmed PC Thomas, "I'm glad I caught you alone. The doctor and nurse are concerned about her injuries. Her bruises aren't consistent with any climbing injury."

"What do you mean exactly?"

"The bruising to her arms is most likely from being grabbed."

"Perhaps her husband grabbed her as he fell," postured the DI.

"But she says she wasn't with him when he fell. And her X-rays show multiple rib fractures that don't tie up with her story of a fall when she was a child. The doctor says although they are healed they are not that old, and they are from multiple incidents, not from a single fall."

"What are you suggesting?"

"I think she was abused."

"By her husband?"

"Yes."

"And what, that she killed him on top of Snowdon?"

"I'm not suggesting that sir no, just that maybe there's more to this case than meets the eye."

"Well I guess we'll have some more questions for Mrs. Jones then."

Just then Sam stepped out of the mortuary and into the corridor where Peter and Rebecca were talking.

"I'd like to go back to the cottage now, if that's OK?"

"Of course," replied Peter, "it is awfully late now and you must be exhausted. Rebecca, can you take Mrs. Jones back to her cottage please."

"Thank you."

"But we will need to ask you some more questions in the morning. Can I have someone pick you up around 10 am?"

"Oh, yes of course."

As soon as Rebecca and Sam had left the hospital Peter placed a call.

"Llanberis MRT, Bryn Davies speaking."

"Hi Bryn, its Peter Constable. Did you all get back OK?"

"Yes mate. All accounted for, nasty accident though. How is the guy's wife holding up?"

"Surprisingly well. Can you describe how you found the body?"

"Can do better than that. I'll send you some photos."

"Thanks. And in your opinion does it definitely look like an accidental fall?"

"Yes. Why do you ask?"

"Oh just the usual paperwork, you know."

"Is there anything else?"

"No thanks Bryn. You better get some rest. I'll see you in the Vaynol soon."

"Right you are, first round's on you I think."

CHAPTER THREE

At exactly 10am the next day Sam heard footsteps on the path alongside the cottage, followed by a sharp knock at the door.

Sam opened the pale blue front door of the cottage to see PC Rebecca Thomas standing on the doorstep, the garden dropping away behind her to a waterfall and stream with the mountain behind that. The air was fresh and the only sound was the rushing of water over rocks in the stream.

"Morning PC Thomas, I didn't expect it would be you," said a surprised Sam.

"I wanted to make sure you're OK and my shift starts at ten anyway, so it was no big deal to start a few minutes early to come up here."

When they arrived at the police station, DI Peter Constable was already waiting for them and had an interview room ready for them.

"Morning Mrs. Jones. How are you feeling today?" started Peter.

"Still a little shaken of course, but not too bad thank you Inspector."

"Can we get you a tea or coffee?"

"Tea please."

"Of course, just give me a minute to sort that."

He stepped out of the room leaving Sam and Rebecca alone.

A few minutes later he returned with a paper cup of hot tea clearly from a vending machine.

He placed the cup down on the table in front of Sam.

"I know this might be difficult but could you just run me through your day yesterday."

"I'll try," started Sam, "we got up and had breakfast, and left the cottage about 8am to catch the bus up to Pen-Y-Pass to start our climb up Snowdon."

"Which path did you take up?"

"Miners I think it was, the one past all the lakes and up all those zig-zag steps."

"Yes, that's the Miners' track. And everything was OK on your way up?"

"Yes. I mean it was hard work and we had to stop for a few breaks, but yes everything was fine. The view over those lakes is stunning, and we had a few snacks with us to have on the way."

"Do you remember what time you reached the

summit?"

"I think we reached the queue for the summit cairn just before 12 and probably queued for about half an hour after that."

"Did you get a photo at the summit?"

"Yes, but it's on my husband's phone."

Sam could see the phone in a sealed evidence bag on the table which the DI had brought in with him when he brought the tea in.

"Of course, we will give that back to you by the way. We just need it for a little longer. Actually do you know his code to unlock it?"

"Yes, it's a pattern one."

Peter removed the phone from the evidence bag on the table breaking the tamper-proof seal and turned it on before sliding it across the table for Sam to unlock.

Sam unlocked the phone while Peter watched her carefully, and pushed it back across the table.

Peter opened the photo gallery and swiped through the most recent photos.

"There's the two of you at the summit. You both look very happy."

"It was quite an achievement, climbing our first mountain together."

"And neither of you had climbed before?"

"No, we'd never climbed a mountain before."

"Who took the photo?"

"I've no idea, the people behind us in the queue. I think they had a foreign accent. Ryan took a photo for the people in front of us. Just seemed to be that's what everyone did."

"Mind if I take a look at some older photos on here?"

"No, of course, whatever you need."

Peter continued his questioning while simultaneously scrolling back through months of photos on Ryan's phone.

"What did you do next, after the summit photo?"

"We got hot chocolates from the café and had a quick look in the shop. And we both used the loo before we headed back down."

"Which route did you take back?"

"We both followed the same route back until the paths split. Then Ryan wanted to do Crib Goch, but I just wanted to come back down Miners. He was insistent he wanted to do a more challenging route, so he said to make my own way down and he'd meet me back at the cottage. Oh God, I should have gone the same way."

"No good thinking like that Mrs. Jones, Crib Goch is a very challenging route even for experienced mountaineers and we could have been pulling two bodies off the mountain last night."

"I must have got lost somewhere though, I slipped

on some really rough ground and ended up on the Pyg track somehow."

"That explains the cuts on your fingers then?" probed the DI.

"Oh yes, I'd not really thought about that, what with everything else going on."

"Doesn't seem significant does it?"

"No, I guess not."

"You're 42 right?"

Sam nodded.

"And how long have you been married?"

Sam thought back to her wedding day. It was a gorgeous sunny day in June attended by just a small group of family and friends. It was then, the happiest day of her life.

Ryan was three years older than her and she looked up to him. It was true that she had fallen down the stairs as a child and her parents had not taken her to hospital. They really didn't have much time for her so Sam was captivated by the attention Ryan gave her.

"Seventeen years," Sam answered.

"Happily?" enquired Peter.

"Yes," Sam lied.

"Well we had our ups and downs like everyone does," she added, in an attempt to bring her answer a little closer to the painful truth.

She had gotten so used to lying about her relationship with Ryan, pretending to everyone they were a happily married couple deeply in love with one another.

Everyone thought that Ryan doted on her and that Sam only ever wanted to spend all her time with him.

Shortly after they were married Ryan's influence over Sam started getting more severe, though she didn't realise what was happening for a while.

Sam only had a small circle of friends and they usually got together once every couple of weeks before Sam and Ryan got married.

One of them would call up and ask Sam to join them on a trip to town to the Karaoke bar or the cocktail lounge, or just Spoons for lunch. But whenever Sam asked Ryan if it was OK to go he would always have something else planned.

Early on he would take her out for dinner or perhaps just order a takeaway so they could have a quiet evening in together with a bottle of wine, or maybe a surprise trip to the cinema depending what was on.

Sam loved that Ryan wanted to spend so much time with her.

After a few months though the promises of a romantic evening together started to become hollow. He would be late home from work or an unexpected get together with his mates would take precedence at the last minute. Whatever the excuse, it would be too late for Sam to join her friends instead and she would be left home alone.

Eventually the girls just stopped calling, figuring that Sam only wanted to spend her time with Ryan now.

Just then Sam's train of thought was interrupted by the sound of Peter's mobile phone ringing.

"Excuse me a moment," he said as he got up and left the room to answer it.

The DI's ringtone was a familiar tune though she couldn't quite place it. Sam found herself tapping out the beat on the table with her fingers after he'd left the room, then suddenly stopped herself as she remembered how Ryan would stare at her disapprovingly whenever she did it. It made her feel like a small child being told off by an overbearing parent.

She started fiddling with the hem of the baggy jumper she was wearing and realised the scratchy fabric was irritating her neck. She pulled it off over her head and dumped it on the floor beside her.

It was one Ryan had chosen for her. Of course it was, Ryan chose all her clothes. He liked to put her in baggy unflattering clothes in bland colours, unless he was taking her out somewhere then he would dress her up like a Barbie doll so he could parade his trophy wife around in front of all his mates, business associates or anyone else who mattered to

Ryan.

Whenever Sam picked up anything she liked then Ryan would tell her it didn't suit her, it wasn't her colour or worse.

Even her underwear had to be plain and boring, unless it was the overly raunchy stuff he wanted her to wear in the bedroom just for him.

DI Peter Constable re-entered the interview room interrupting Sam's train of thought once again.

She placed her thumb under the strap of her off-white boring bra and lifted it back on to her shoulder, rolling her eyes as she did it.

"Is the temperature OK for you?" enquired Peter noticing that Sam had taken off her jumper but not that she had dumped it on the floor.

"I'm fine thanks."

"So what is it you do for a living Mrs. Jones?"

"I guess you'd just say I'm a housewife," replied Sam.

Before she met Ryan she was working part-time in a little craft shop in the town where she grew up. You would probably describe her as quite introvert and she didn't make friends easily, the few she did have she had known for years.

But in the little shop she found it easy to talk to customers, enjoying the tales from little old ladies knitting socks for their first grandchildren, or what creative costume ideas the young mothers were making for their little ones' first school play; or the mums whose children were now at secondary school and had found a new career for themselves making cute little bookmarks, finger puppets and other trinkets for sale on Etsy or such like.

She met Ryan on a night out with the girls in the nearest big town and his house was on the outskirts. When she moved in with him, it wasn't so easy to get back to her home town, to the little craft shop, and the pay hardly covered the cost of getting there and back each day.

When they got married Ryan persuaded Sam to give the job she loved so much up, with a promise that he would provide for her and take care of her, and that she could live a life of luxury at home.

She had visions of becoming a stay-at-home mum, but sadly that wasn't to be.

"And do you or your husband have any life insurance policies or did you take out travel insurance for your holiday?"

"No," replied Sam, a little surprised by the question, "Ryan hated having to pay the car insurance, he didn't believe in it - said they never pay out, just lining the pockets of the fat cats."

"So with your husband sadly gone, you've no source of income to fall back on?"

"I hadn't really thought about it, but no."

Peter paused for a bit, reviewing the case notes he had in front of him.

"We still need the results from a full post mortem, but the preliminary findings concur with our initial thoughts, that Ryan sadly fell while trying to descend Crib Goch alone in difficult conditions and cracked his skull on a rock where he landed causing a massive brain haemorrhage."

"Oh God," Sam cried, sinking her face in to her hands.

Rebecca leaned forwards, pulling a tissue from the box on the table and passing it to Sam.

"What this means Mrs. Jones," continued Peter, "is that we're no longer treating your husband's death as suspicious and there will be no criminal investigation into the circumstances surrounding his death. You understand that, right?"

Sam nodded silently in agreement.

"With that said," Peter continued softly, "I would like to know how you got those bruises."

Sam swallowed a lump in her throat.

She couldn't remember the first time Ryan had grabbed her by the arm but it was probably when they were out together one evening. It can't have been a posh do as she must have been wearing something with long sleeves so the marks wouldn't show. It was probably in the pub with his mates and Ryan thought some guy was getting a bit close or something so he forcefully manoeuvred her away.

She remembered the last time though, it was two

days ago in Llanberis as they were walking through the village centre and Ryan suddenly decided they would cross the road. He grabbed her forearm really tight leaving a mark still visible the next day and dragged her across the road like she was a petulant child.

"I'm not sure it really matters now Inspector," Sam admitted quietly.

"I guess you're right, if there's nothing you'd like us to investigate," replied Peter.

Suddenly Sam went pale in her face as she remembered the worst time Ryan had beaten her.

Ryan didn't want children and he was insistent she took the pill, religiously popping each one out of the blister pack every night and watching to make sure she took it.

But nothing is fool proof and a bout of diarrhoea had stopped it working one month and Sam fell unexpectedly pregnant.

Sam kept her suspicions of being pregnant secret at first and kept taking the pill but a few days after taking a pregnancy test to confirm it, Ryan found the positive test in the bathroom bin which Sam had forgotten to empty.

He was furious, blaming it all on Sam of course and stormed out in a blinding rage. He came back hours later, completely drunk and still the angriest he'd ever been.

Sam tried in vain to calm him down, assuring

him that everything would be OK, that she'd take complete care of the baby and nothing would change between the two of them.

Nothing worked and Ryan punched Sam in the stomach.

A few days later Sam suffered a miscarriage.

She dealt with it entirely by herself having nobody she could turn to.

A week later she plucked up the courage to tell Ryan, thinking he would be happy there would be no baby but instead he berated her with, "You can't even do that right."

"Are you OK Mrs. Jones?" asked a genuinely concerned Peter Constable.

"Yes, I think I just need to go home now."

"Of course. Again I am so sorry for your loss, but you are free to go. Do you have anyone you can call? A friend perhaps?"

"I'll call my friend Karen when I get back to the cottage. Thank you."

"PC Thomas will give you a lift back."

CHAPTER FOUR

It was not long after the pregnancy scare that Ryan told Sam she was looking fat and she should go to the gym.

That would turn out to be the best thing he ever said to her as that is where she met Karen.

Every Tuesday evening Sam would get to go out for a few hours and have some time away from Ryan and away from the virtual prison that was their house.

She caught sight of Karen on a rowing machine across the gym on her very first visit.

Karen was slim with long dark hair and always looked great in her neon coloured zip-front sports bra and tight fitting Lycra leggings, which Sam imagined she probably wore everywhere and not just to the gym. Ryan would never let her wear anything like that.

Sam also imagined that if she was in to girls that she would most definitely be in to Karen.

Sam was trying to figure out the controls on the treadmill when a female voice surprised her, and she looked up from the bemusing control panel of the machine to see the neon and Lycra clad woman now standing right next to her.

"Hi. I'm Karen, not seen you in here before."

"Er, no," stuttered Sam, "a gym virgin."

"So what are you here for?" enquired Karen cheerfully.

"To lose some weight," replied Sam nervously.

Karen grabbed either side of Sam's loose fitting T-shirt and stretched it across her tummy.

"Who are you kidding, you look gorgeous, you lose much weight and you'll be virgin' on the ridiculous", she laughed.

Sam laughed too. She couldn't remember the last time she had laughed properly before that.

"It's this baggy top you're wearing that's the problem."

Why are you here, Sam thought to herself? But then it dawned on her that perhaps the gym was why Karen looked as good as she did.

"You don't need the treadmill, you need to build some muscle tone; you want to do some weights or rowing and get those skinny arms working."

"Um, OK," agreed Sam reluctantly as she followed Karen across the gym to a weights bench.

Every Tuesday the two women met in the gym for a couple of hours of workouts then had enough time for a coffee and a brief chat in the leisure centre café before Sam had to get back home to avoid Ryan becoming suspicious.

"Any kids at home?" Karen enquired.

"No," Sam replied softly.

"Just the hubby, then?" Karen quizzed, glancing down at the ring on Sam's left ring finger.

Sam nodded with a forced smile.

"Still waiting for mine. Three years we've been together and he still hasn't asked, but truth be told we're happy as we are really."

For the first time in years Sam had a friend to talk to.

But she remained guarded and couldn't tell Karen the truth about her life with Ryan. Karen would become the one person that knew Sam better than anyone in the world, but she couldn't know everything.

CHAPTER FIVE

Once PC Rebecca Thomas had dropped Sam back at the cottage, she called her only friend, Karen, "There's been an accident climbing Snowdon."

"Oh God, are you OK?" insisted a shocked Karen immediately.

"Yes, I'm OK, its Ryan. He fell..."

"And is he OK?"

"No," Sam responded quietly, "he died on the mountain."

"My God, are you sure you're OK?" Karen pressed once again, "Where are you?"

"Yes, yes, I'm OK. I'm still at the cottage. I'm driving home tomorrow, can we catch up when I'm back?"

"Yes of course, just let me know when you're back and I'll be right there."

Sam packed her clothes neatly in the suitcase except for what she would wear for the drive home tomorrow, her toothbrush and wash bag.

She stuffed Ryan's clothes into a bin bag from the kitchen drawer; this year's shirt from his favourite football team, designer shirts, expensive trainers, the lot.

She made herself dinner and sat alone at the dining table as she ate and drank her way through a bottle of White Zinfandel, occasionally glancing at the stuffed black bin bag across the room, the only thing left of Ryan in sight.

After clearing away her dinner things and tidying the cottage so all she would have to do in the morning was strip the bed and load the car up, she headed to bed for her second night alone since getting married. She slept exceptionally well.

The next morning Sam started the 300 plus mile journey to home near the south coast of England, stopping at the picturesque riverside village of Betws-Y-Coed a little less than an hour into her journey.

She pulled up outside a little village store and crossed the road to a charity clothing collection bin, and forced the bag of Ryan's possessions through the narrow opening.

She crossed back and went in to the little store where she bought a bottle of locally distilled orange marmalade gin which she had tried in the local pub a few nights previously.

"Karen would love this," she thought to herself as she tapped her debit card on the pin pad with a smile.

She then continued the long drive home, stopping only once more for fuel and a coffee at an anonymous motorway services somewhere on the M40.

Without Ryan's phone which he usually used to stream his favourite music in the car, Sam was left to hop between radio stations as she drove in and out of signal coverage, skipping the ones she didn't fancy, and settling on those playing the kind of music she liked.

She particularly liked the romantic rock ballads of the 1980s and some up to date pop artists. She never cared much for Ryan's choice of hard rock and depressing 90s and early 2000s "slit your wrists" tracks that were usually staple listening for him.

It was a long and solitary journey along seemingly never-ending ribbons of black bitumen asphalt winding their way through the Welsh and English countryside.

Sam felt herself tiring of the long drive by the time she reached the M25 around London, but the dreaded rumble of the infamous concrete slab section through Surrey sharply disrupted her tiredness, and ensured she stayed awake for the home stretch.

CHAPTER SIX

As soon as she got back she called Karen, who appeared at the door just ten minutes later. When the door opened Karen immediately flung her arms around Sam and gave her a huge bear hug.

Karen was wearing a gorgeous pale green dress and looked just as great as she did in her gym gear.

"So you don't just wear Lycra then," joked Sam.

"And this is what your house looks like," retorted Karen, both making subtle reference to the fact they'd never seen one another beyond the bounds of the leisure centre car park before.

Sam mixed two glasses of the newly purchased marmalade gin, placing them together with the gin and lemonade bottles on the coffee table before sinking into the sofa next to Karen.

"Ooh this is good stuff," remarked Karen, "it won't take long to get drunk on this."

"I've got something to tell you," Sam started seriously after downing her first glass of gin for

Dutch courage, "Ryan used to beat me."

"Well about time," snapped Karen flinging her arms around Sam once again and giving her the biggest squeeze.

"What do you mean?" uttered a bemused Sam, "Did you know?"

"Samantha Bethany Macintosh", Karen berated her playfully, referencing her full maiden name like a parent does when telling off a child. "I've been your best friend for eight years, of course I knew something wasn't right and I've seen the bruises you hide. But I knew I couldn't push you. I've been waiting patiently for you to tell me in your own time."

Sam had tried to tell her own mother once, but she had dismissed the idea completely.

"You're being silly love, it's clear Ryan loves you, he just doesn't know his own strength that's all," her mother had proclaimed when Sam showed her one of the countless bruises he'd left from grabbing her forcefully by the arm.

From that day on she felt truly alone in the world and didn't think she could trust anyone else to tell what was really happening to her. After all if her own mother didn't believe her, who else would?

It was like Karen had lifted a great dam and all the pain and suffering now came flooding out as Sam retold the years of mental and physical abuse she'd endured from Ryan.

The stories were punctuated by waves of uncontrollable tears from Sam and impromptu squeezy hugs from Karen.

Finally as the bottle of gin was nearly empty Sam came to the day of the climb.

It was Karen who had first gotten Sam into climbing four years ago.

"You should come on the climbing wall," Karen suggested in the café after gym one week, "I go every Thursday."

"Oh I'd love to, but I'm busy on Thursdays," Sam lied, knowing that Ryan would not want to let her out more than one night a week, "Tuesday is pretty much the only night I have free."

"Well let's do it next Tuesday then, I'll just switch my gym day. Your first climb is free if you come as my guest, I think you'll be good at it."

The climbing wall was in the leisure centre, so the next week they met up as usual in the reception but instead of heading for the weights and rowing machines in the gym they put on harnesses and headed for the artificial rock face that towered two storeys high just inside the front of the steel and glass faced building.

"You're a natural," shouted Karen from the bottom as Sam reached the top of her first route in record time.

From then on, apart from the occasional trip to

the gym, they spent every Tuesday evening scaling the heights of the man-made indoor mountain ranges and practicing their bouldering techniques.

Her gym membership could easily be extended to include the climbing wall, so Ryan would not know when he trawled the bank statements of their joint account.

"You're so lucky," Karen screamed with genuine jealousy when Sam told her she and Ryan were going to climb Snowdon, "my other half would rather just sit in front of his big screen TV watching the footy than take me to climb a mountain. Ask your hubby if there's room for one more?" pleaded Sam's secret friend.

If only Karen knew why Sam couldn't possibly ask Ryan if she could come too, though in hindsight now perhaps she did know and wasn't asking just out of jealousy but out of fear for her best friend's safety.

Sam relayed the day's events in detail.

They had prepared their backpacks the night before with high energy snacks, a woolly hat and sun hat, waterproof coat and trousers, sunglasses, sun hat, sun cream, map, compass and whistle.

In the morning they started early with porridge for breakfast, before putting two bottles of water each in their bags and left the cottage around 8am.

They flagged down a passing bus at the stop just across the road from the narrow wooden bridge that crossed the stream to the little cottage.

They got off with everyone else at Pen-Y-Pass and started the long climb along the Miners track.

It was busy so Ryan was on his best behaviour, he would never mistreat Sam in public, not if he thought anyone was looking anyway.

The path is fairly gentle as it meanders round the lakes and reservoirs on the lower slopes of the mountain, before joining the Pyg track and climbing the famously steep zig-zag steps, eventually joining the Llanberis, Snowdon Ranger and Crib Goch paths for the last section to the summit station.

Then they joined the thirty to forty minute long queue on the steps to the summit cairn, for the obligatory summit photo.

Ryan became visibly agitated after a few minutes of standing in the line but not wanting to embarrass himself amongst the tightly packed crowd of tourists he said nothing.

When it was their turn Ryan unlocked his phone and passed it to the man behind them in the queue to take a few pictures.

Ryan smiled, probably just because it was the right thing to do. Sam smiled with joy at conquering her first real mountain climb, with a slight smirk in one photo as she thought about how jealous Karen must be right now.

After their summit photos they headed back down to the summit station to get a hot drink, browse the shop quickly and visit the loo.

So far Sam's recollection of the day matched exactly with how she had relayed it to the police back in Wales.

Then they began their descent back down the mountain, with Sam leading the way.

"Which way now love?" called Ryan cheerfully as they approached the large vertical stone that marked the point where the paths diverged once more, with really no idea himself where they were going.

A slightly smaller stone marked the direction of the Llanberis path straight ahead and the Snowdon Ranger path to the left but there was no sign for the Miners track they had come up.

"This way," replied Sam confidently as she led the way onwards slightly to the right of the Llanberis path but missing the top of the zig-zag steps they had climbed up earlier.

"Are you sure?"

"Yes, it's definitely this way", she called back as she strode off into the distance away from the crowds.

Before too long they had reached the precarious knife-edged ridge of Crib Goch.

They could see nobody coming up the ridge and nobody ever climbed down this route.

"Well done genius," Ryan berated Sam, only once he was sure there was nobody else within earshot, "trust you to get us lost on a bloody mountain, well done indeed," barging past Sam and almost knocking her down. "I'll lead now shall I?" he asked rhetorically.

It was one of the things he did to belittle her, force her to make a decision only to then punish her somehow later for making the wrong one.

Like the time he asked her to pick somewhere to go for dinner and she chose a Mexican restaurant she'd heard good things about from Karen.

Sam thought they'd had a wonderful time and really enjoyed her food, and Ryan had been the perfect gentleman all evening at the restaurant and on the way home.

But as soon as the front door of their house closed behind him, Ryan lunged at Sam and she took a severe beating.

"You know I don't like Mexican food, you stupid little girl!" he yelled angrily.

Sam had no idea he didn't like Mexican food, they'd just never had it before, but she knew next time he asked, only to suggest places they had actually been to before.

Back on the mountain the clouds were starting to close in around them and Ryan lost his footing on some loose rock.

He recovered himself though and carried on.

"That's the last time I listen to any decisions you make," he shouted out in front of him, continuing along the treacherous ridge, without turning around to see how his wife was coping.

Sam of course with her experience on the climbing wall back home was doing absolutely fine.

That's the last time I listen to you, Sam thought to herself as she picked up a large rock at her feet.

It weighed about 1.5 kilos and had a sharp edge along one side. With all her might Sam plunged the sharp edge of the rock into the back of Ryan's skull and he fell instantly.

She checked for a pulse and there wasn't one, blood now starting to ooze from the wound on the back of his head.

Sam dragged her husband's body quickly by his arms to the top of a boulder jutting out of the mountainside a short distance away and rolled his lifeless corpse over the edge.

She grabbed the rock she had struck him with and placed it carefully under his head so it would look like he had cracked his skull when he landed on it.

She rinsed her hands in a nearby stream and then used the empty water bottle from her back pack to collect water from the stream and wash Ryan's blood away from the higher path. The forecast bad weather overnight would remove the rest but it would be good enough so whomever found him would not notice.

Sam put the water bottle back in her bag, slung it over her shoulders and carefully continued her descent.

She knew climbing down Crib Goth was incredibly dangerous, but either way, even if she died up here herself, she would be rid of Ryan.

Of course with four years of solid training alongside Karen on the climbing wall, she got down with ease.

The path off Crib Goch meets the Pyg track just before the car park so anyone seeing her at the bottom would just think she had descended the much easier Pyg track.

She hopped on the next bus back to the cottage, and made herself a hot chocolate.

As she sunk back into the comfy sofa with the large mug in her hand, Sam smiled, realising the mountain had finally set her free.

Karen put her arms around her best friend once more, squeezing her tighter than ever.

"You poor thing," she said softly, "at least you're safe now, but what did the police say?"

"The doctors alerted the PC who took me to the hospital, I think her name was Rebecca, to some of the bruises Ryan had given me. They took X-Rays and found I had some broken ribs from where Ryan punched me."

"Ryan broke your ribs, I never knew that, if I thought it was that bad I'd have said something sooner," interjected Karen.

"It's not your fault, I kept it all hidden, you weren't to know. Anyway I'm sure they didn't believe my story about how I got the broken ribs. They asked if I wanted to have them look into it further, but I said no."

"So what are they doing now, I mean are they going to come after you?"

"No, they said it was an accident and they wouldn't be investigating further."

"Wow. I guess you're really lucky in the end then, don't worry you're secret is safe with me."

"I knew it would be, thank you so much for being here."

"Of course, that's what best friends are for. You don't have to ever think about that horrible man ever again… Just one question though…"

"What?"

"Where did you get that gin? We need some more of that."

ACKNOWLEDGEMENT

This is my fourth book, and the first to be set outside of Cornwall.

Escape on Yr Wyddfa was inspired by an amazing family holiday in Summer 2023 to the stunning Eryri National Park (Snowdonia).

After months of training on the South Downs near our home, my wife Nichola, our two kids Isabel and Jack, and our young Cocker Spaniel Benji, spent a week in a little cottage very similar to the one in the story at the foot of Yr Wyddfa (Snowdon). I am immensely proud of my family for climbing the mountain with me and I am very grateful for them supporting my writing efforts.

I would also like to thank the many people of North Wales who made our stay so enjoyable.

PRAISE FOR AUTHOR

Comments about previous books by the author.

"Can highly recommend this short story. I'm not a reader usually (very rare) but read it all in just ONE SITTING as I wanted to find out what happened next!"

"I was totally immersed in the story and could picture each bit... I even shed a tear at the last bit ... how lovely. Can't wait for your next book."

"Loved this book. Perfect for a cosy Sunday afternoon read. The author did a great job of making it have enough suspense and intrigue without dragging it out and making it too plot twisty!"

"Received this afternoon, started, finished and thoroughly enjoyed this evening. Bravo, can't wait for the next one."

BOOKS BY THIS AUTHOR

Ashton: Escaping The Island

A young woman on the run with nothing but a newborn baby and a heavy denim bag tries desperately to stay safe.

We first meet her on an unfamiliar street beside a quiet harbour, cold and scared, with no idea where to turn next.

Their challenging journey is set in rural south-west Cornwall and a fictional island located off the far tip of England.

This debut short story from new author Paul Young is sure to keep you guessing from the opening scene to the thrilling finale.

Mila: Return To The Island

Two years after the end of Ashton: Escaping the

Island, little Mila is preparing for her first day at school.

Ashton, Louisa and Mila have settled in to rural life in Cornwall and the events of the first book are a distant memory.

But a new drama soon rocks the little extended family to the core and a hunt across Dartmoor, Cornwall and beyond soon ensues.

Can they really go through another torturous situation?
Relative newcomer, Paul Young, keeps you guessing again with this thrilling sequel.

Louisa: Revenge Of The Island

No matter how hard they all try, their connection to the mysterious island still haunts them.

Is it really possible to stay away forever?

Or will The Island have revenge on our trio in the end?

This gripping conclusion to The Island Mysteries trilogy explores the Island's influence on different characters and takes a much darker turn.

SEEKING HELP

If you have been affected by any part of this story please reach out to your friends, family or a support organisation for help.

In the UK, the charity Refuge run the National Domestic Abuse Helpline for women suffering any kind of domestic abuse, available 24 hours a day.

UK Freephone 0808 2000 247

They also offer an online live chat service at: www.nationaldahelpline.org.uk

Men can also suffer domestic abuse but can find it even harder to talk about it. Respect is a charity that run a free helpline for male victims of domestic abuse.

UK Freephone 0808 8010327

Their website is at: mensadviceline.org.uk

Printed in Great Britain
by Amazon